LET'S TALK ABOUT IT:

Stepfamilies

FRED ROGERS

PHOTOGRAPHS BY JIM JUDKIS

G. P. PUTNAM'S SONS · NEW YORK

Special thanks to Hedda Bluestone Sharapan on our staff for research and development; to the consultants whom we've met through Stepfamily Association of America, Emily Visher, Ph.D., and Elizabeth Einstein, M.A.; and to our friends who shared their personal and professional experiences with us.

Special thanks also to the children, parents, and stepparents who are seen in the portraits below. Their photographs appear throughout the book. We're especially grateful to them for their help and enthusiastic participation.

Text and photographs copyright © 1997 by Family Communications, Inc. All rights reserved.
This book, or parts thereof, may not be reproduced in any form without permission in writing from
the publisher. G. P. Putnam's Sons, a division of The Putnam & Grosset Group,
200 Madison Avenue, New York, NY 10016. G. P. Putnam's Sons, Reg. U.S. Pat. & Tm. Off.
Published simultaneously in Canada. Printed in Singapore. Project Director: Margy Whitmer
Designed by Jackie Schuman and Donna Mark. Text set in Korinna
Library of Congress Cataloging-in-Publication Data Rogers, Fred, Stepfamilies / Fred Rogers;
photographs by Jim Judkis. p. cm. — (Let's talk about it / Fred Rogers) Summary:
Discusses the changes involved in becoming part of a stepfamily and ways to deal with
the new situation. 1. Stepfamilies — Juvenile literature. 2. Stepchildren — Juvenile literature.
[1. Stepfamilies.] I. Judkis, Jim, ill II. Title. III. Series: Rogers, Fred.
Let's talk about it. HQ759.92.R64 1997 646.7'8 — dc20 96-34176 CIP AC
ISBN 0-399-23144-7 (hc)
1   3   5   7   9   10   8   6   4   2
ISBN 0-399-23145-5 (pbk)
1   3   5   7   9   10   8   6   4   2
First Impression

As we were working on this book, we came to have real empathy for everyone in stepfamilies. While there's a sense of a fresh start, new beginnings, there are also a lot of complicated feelings about changes and relationships which need to be carefully considered.

A man and a woman begin a stepfamily with all sorts of loving hopes and dreams of what "could be." Of course, some of those images are realistic and some aren't. The children who are part of that new family bring feelings from what "has been." Some of those feelings come from strong, deep and loving bonds. So, naturally, it's hard for them to form new bonds while holding on to what's important to them from their past. Becoming comfortable with new "others" takes time and understanding.

No matter what the situation, if we can help children talk about their concerns and their feelings (and really listen to what they tell us), we are letting them know we care deeply about them. Whatever is mentionable can be more manageable. That's why we named this series "Let's Talk About It." It's an invitation for you and your child to take what we offer and talk about it in your own ways...ways that feel right for you and your family.

Changes can be hard, but if we can deal with them caringly and openly, we can become stronger and closer to the ones we love. Lasting relationships aren't built overnight. I wish you well as you and your children grow into being "family."

Fred Rogers

Changes are a part of everyone's life.

You already know about changes...changes in your own life. Little by little, you get used to changes and new ways of doing things.

Knowing that can often help you feel strong inside.

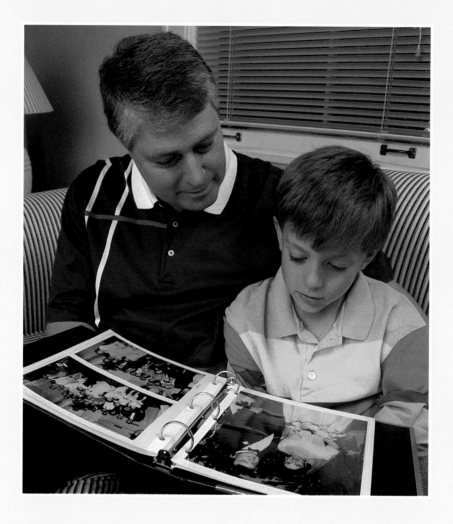

When your mom or dad remarries and you become part of a stepfamily, there are usually many changes. Some changes can be really hard, especially at first. Everyone needs time to get used to those changes and to try to understand what this new family is about—even the grownups.

There might be changes in where you live, or where you go on weekends, or even where you go to school. You might also have to share a room with a stepbrother or stepsister.

Your place in the family might also change. You might now be the oldest child or the youngest or in the middle.

Sometimes it might seem like there are too many changes.

Children can have lots of feelings about being in a stepfamily. Sometimes you might feel left out or jealous. You might remember times when you had your mom or dad to yourself. Now you have to share your parent with the other people in your new family. You might feel sad and wish things were the way they used to be, but wishing doesn't make things happen—not good things or bad things.

If you feel bad because now your mom or dad doesn't spend as much time with you as you'd like, you can talk about that, and together, you might be able to work out some special time for just the two of you.

At first, you might wonder how you're going to like your new stepparent and the other people in your stepfamily, but the way you feel in the beginning may not be the way you'll feel later on. It takes time to get to know people...even people you live with.

You might even be surprised to know that other people in your stepfamily have some of the same feelings you do. You're all trying to figure out what your new family is all about. Everyone might be wondering, "What's my place in this family?"

There are times when you might have some confusing feelings about your parents and your stepparents. Some children wonder how their mother will feel if they love their stepmother, and some wonder how their father will feel if they love their stepfather.

Well, just because you love one person doesn't mean you can't love someone else. You have many different kinds of love inside you—love for the people in your family, love for your friends, your teachers... your pets.

When you're part of a stepfamily, you may not like some of the new ways of doing things. But families make rules to help people get along with one another and know what to expect.

All through your life, you find out that different people have different ways of doing things. One way may not be better than another, just different.

Talking about the new rules with someone you love can help you get used to them.

Another thing to get used to is that your stepparent will help take care of you. Sometimes that stepparent might ask you to do something you don't want to do.

Children might say, "You're not my real
mother," or "You're not my real father." Then
a stepparent could answer, "You may be
angry right now, but I care about you, and
as you know, that's how we do things in
this family."

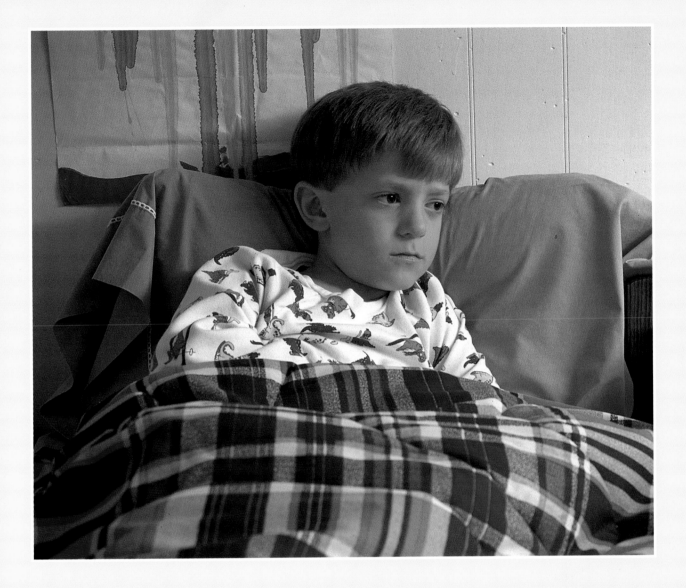

Most people find that some changes are easy to make and some are really hard. That's how it is in all families.

People don't know what you're thinking or feeling unless you tell them. If you can talk about things that make you happy, sad, or angry, your parents and the other people in your stepfamily can better understand what you're feeling. Sometimes they can even make changes that are really helpful.

Playing can help, too. You might want to draw pictures or play with puppets or make up stories. When you're upset or angry, there are many things you can do that don't hurt you or anybody else.

Even though it may not be easy to be part of a new family, as you spend time together, you might find you're feeling more and more comfortable with one another.

Stepbrothers and stepsisters can become new friends, too. There can be times when you talk together, play together and laugh together.

By doing things together, you'll be making
memories that will always be special about
your new family.

All the people in your life are important to
who you are.

As time goes on and you get used to your stepfamily, you'll probably see how much you're learning about people...and families... and about yourself.

Isn't it great to find out that there are many people, of all ages, who care about you,

and many people you can care about, too!